WARNING

* * * * * * * * * * * * * * * * * * *

WANT FREE COPIES OF MY BOOKS?
Just visit my blog and download free copies of my books:
http://gideon-elliot.awesomeauthors.org/gideon-elliot/

About the Publisher

4Fun Publishing, a member of **BLVNP Incorporated**, 340 S. Lemon #6200, Walnut CA 91789, info@blvnp.com / legal@blvnp.com
NOTE: Due to the highly emotional reaction of some people to works of erotic fiction, any email sent to the above address that contains foul language or religious references is automatically deleted by our anti-spam software and will not be seen. All other communications are welcome.

DISCLAIMER

Please don't be stupid and kill yourself. This book is a work of FICTION. Do not try any new sexual practice that you find in this book. It is fiction and not to be confused with reality. Neither the author nor the publisher or its associates assume any responsibility for any loss, injury, death or legal consequences resulting from acting on the contents in this book. Every character in this book is over 18 years of age. The author's opinions are not to be construed as the opinions of the publisher. The material in this book is for entertainment purposes ONLY. Enjoy.

GIDEON ELLIOT

TABOO EROTICA

HYPNOTIZED

3 IN 1 BOXED SET

Hypnotized
3-in-1 Boxed Set
Taboo Erotica

By: Gideon Elliot

ISBN: 978-1-62761-588-4

TABLE OF CONTENTS

GIDEON ELLIOT

Gay Hypnotic Submission Erotica

SHIFTING POWER

I'D KNOWN Jason since we were kids. I've always admired him – so much that it sometimes overwhelmed me. My admiration began with the way he looked. I always just enjoyed seeing him. He was a scrawny kid at the pool in the summertime, but lithe. He was adorable. When I think of him now, as I remember him during the summer, many years ago, when we were both seven, I can still see him as we undressed in the bungalow our families shared in Rockaway. He looked, stretching himself out of his little wet speedo, like nothing so much as a plucked chicken.

In his early teens he was smart and snappy and thoughtful, dressed sharp, got into gym and working out, as well as folk music – he taught himself guitar -- film noir, the Marquis de Sade, differential calculus, Nietzsche, and automobile engines. Girls talked about him, giggling with desire. He was easy around them, affectionate, cuddly, and, although he dated, he never got tied down to one girl friend. But none of the girls he dated expected him to, and none of them lacked for dates with other guys.

What was really beautiful is that he allowed me to love him. He was glad to accept it; he didn't push me away. When I looked at him with wondering eyes, with helpless admiration, he just grabbed me by the shoulder and horsed around for a minute.

Then he'd smile in the friendliest way. I didn't feel the least bit ashamed for showing my devotion. I'm always at ease with him but there are moments when I feel the excitement shaking inside me like I do with no one else. He's noticed it. And he doesn't hold it against me.

He'd go nuts if he couldn't accept love, 'cause he's a guy that everybody's crazy about, and he even can stay friends with girls who are dying for him but he won't sleep with them.

***

WE WERE in Butler library. We were seventeen. It was after ten, and the place was relatively empty. I'd managed to read all of Mill's *On Liberty* and I was thinking about the various possible extents and limits of human responsibility. I didn't get anyplace solid in my thought. I was spacey, floating, feeling like I was thinking but unable, the next moment, to remember exactly what I had been thinking.

Suddenly I heard fingers snap in front of my face and I saw Jason grinning. He'd just finished an assignment in differential calculus. If I had just had to squeeze my brain into that mold for two hours, I would not have been smiling.

"Where are you, Buddy?"

"I'm thinking about the limits of social responsibility and how you determine how much control any person can put on another; or an abstract group, like society, on the individual."

"Did anyone ever tell you that you lose yer bloom when you think."

"Cut the shit," I said, laughing at how beautifully he could move me from one place to another without even noticing it. "Aren't you tired of calculus already?" I said. "You're thinking all the time, and you haven't lost your bloom."

"Let's get some coffee," he said, throwing his arm round my shoulders.

"And stay up all night?"

"Don't worry."

Well, when Jason says "don't worry," you don't worry.

I couldn't get enough of him. I suppressed my sexual desire in order to be able to keep being with him. He didn't mind how I felt, but still I didn't want to make him uncomfortable by putting him in the awkward position of feeling like demands were being made on him, or of seeming like he was rejecting me. Most of the time it worked. I forgot about how much I wanted him and just enjoyed being with him the way we were. I forgot my sexual desire, or maybe it lingered as a ground bass giving greater resonance to whatever we did. I had become like an anorexic. Something else was more important to me than eating.

Oh, but in my secret heart, I wanted him to long for me as much as I longed for him. I idolized him, and I wanted him to sanctify that feeling, not just accept it. I started to scheme. I'd always been turned on by hypnotism. You will do as I say – that kind of stuff -- since I'm a kid.

I wanted him, *that way*. And I began to think he wanted me like that, too, but he wasn't able to get in touch with that feeling and see himself feeling that way. I knew that was true. I had to get him to acknowledge it.

I still idolized him. Even more. Just because he had that failing. He was holding himself back. I could help him. I'd use myself, use myself, for him, not for myself. I would serve him. I'd bring him out, bring him closer to me, make him grateful to me the way I felt grateful to him just for looking at me.

I went on scheming.

***

THE WAKE trailed behind the ferry. The sky was clear. Jason was pulling Amy close to him. They were exchanging little pecking kisses like birds and staring, lost in each other's eyes. I saw this, but I didn't look long. My thoughts were absorbed in formless longing that breasted and flattened like the waves around the boat.

Staten Island is always disappointing and we went right back to Manhattan. The trip was rendered hilarious when a pigeon landed on a woman's hat. We assured each other we actually had seen it. The pigeon landed on her hat and she flinched and it whizzed away with a flump of its feathers.

"She didn't treat him nicely when he was dying."

We were sitting in a café near South Ferry.

"I told her so," Amy continued.

"Did she respond?"

"She whined 'What should I do?' 'Just be nice' I said. 'Why?' she asked. 'He's dying.' I said. 'His last minutes should be happy.' 'What does it matter?' she said. 'They won't last long,' I said. But she said, 'exactly, and then, no matter what, they won't matter to him cause there'll be no him for them to matter to.'"

"She's tough," Jason said.

"She's cruel," I said.

"She got what she wanted," Amy said

"Uh-huh," Jason said.

"I'm afraid of you," I said, as if joking.

***

I COULD have predicted it. Amy dumped Jason. No girl had ever done that to him, before. There must have been a reason, but he wouldn't say. He spent a lot of time hanging around my place just being tense, depressed and irritable. Even I, who loved him with such a self-suppressing love that I would have given my life for him, I even began to feel myself losing patience with him.

Several times I felt anger rise within me against him. What surprised me was that I was able to hold back from expressing that anger or even experiencing it. I dismissed it, refused to grant it sway over me, and that gave me strength I had not thought was mine in every area. I needed less sleep, less food, and more physical activity. I started going back to the gym – weight routines and swimming. I was vibrant. For the first time in my life, Jason noticed me. He sounded angry.

"What the fuck is this? I'm losing it and suddenly you're looking…"

I smiled, and his good nature came back and he finished the sentence with a grin… "incredible."

"Thanks," I said.

"What's your secret?"

"No secret," I said, lying. "Maybe 'cause I've been going to the gym and working out regularly."

"Maybe I should go with you."

"Come on," I said, delighted.

It was just what I wanted. I kept on scheming.

It was fun going to the gym with Jason. My routine wasn't just for me anymore, so that I could look good. It was a performance for him, undertaken with a care for grace and presentation as well as an exercise in strength, focus, and precision. I loved it when he looked at me. He got into the spirit, and I knew he was showing off for me, and enjoying it, too. But that wasn't enough for me. I had to have him admit something, desire something, the sexuality of another man. But he wasn't ready for that, I thought.

I had more scheming to do.

Jason had another fault. This one was even more serious than his private betrayal of his sexual self by keeping it hidden and forbidden. He had turned his degree in Mathematics into a high paying job designing next-generation weaponry for Latent Technologies, which was heavily funded by the U.S. government and was just inches away from being a branch of the CIA. This was a betrayal of his private self, an abdication of his social responsibility, and a betrayal of his discipline. But he wouldn't hear any talk about it. "I play with numbers," he'd say, and that was the end of the conversation.

I wanted to take control of his mind and dominate his will and make him be exactly as I wanted him to be. And I wanted him to know that he was mine and be glad of it. But how the hell was I going to accomplish that? Oh, yes, I know, I mentioned hypnosis before. I wish! I'm not so good at it, and besides how could I ever get Jason to a place where I'd even be able to try to hypnotize him. It would be much easier if he already were hypnotized.

And then one night some angel of possibility blew in my ear and I just asked him if he'd ever been hypnotized. He was stretched out on the couch reading *Scientific American*. The question wasn't that far out of left-field because we'd seen the old John Huston movie *Freud* the night before. And we'd laughed through the scene where Montgomery Clift hypnotizes a young and pretty David McCallum, who is hysterically embracing a dress maker's dummy with all the violent passion buried within him, as if the dummy were his mother.

Jason looked up and said no.

"You want to try it?" I asked.

Jason laughed and with good-natured interest said, "Sure."

I felt myself becoming powerful as I began the induction. My voice was husky and it was dusky and it was enfolding Jason in a dark, sleepy cloud. As my breath wove itself into an incantation I felt my desire for him increase. I began to be hard. I wanted to put my hands on him, to touch him, to feel his muscles, his bones, his skin, his lips. I felt myself closing around him. I felt him becoming more dependent on me. He was under, he was mine.

"Open your eyes," I said.

He sat there looking dazed and blank and ready to obey.

"Take off your shirt," I said.

He did.

"Now stand and pose for me."

He did.

"Now order me to do the same thing."

"Take off your shirt," he said.

I did.

"Now stand and pose for me."

I did.

"Tell me you want to gaze at me," I said.

"I want to gaze at you."

"Tell me you want to give me orders that you want to tell me what to do and see me obey you."

"I want to give you orders and tell you what to do and see you obey me."

"Tell me to get on my knees and worship your cock."

I licked the sweet sensitive inner skin of his cock slit and my eyes rolled back into my head under my closed lids. My breathing was deep and liquid and I was bathing his cock in saliva, taking it all the way to the back of my throat, never having been this content before, filled up now as I was by him, my master, my slave. I couldn't tell which.

"I want to belong to you," he said.

With those words, a bolt of lightning shot through him. He trembled and shook. He stiffened and recoiled and sent his whiplash of seed deep into me.

End of the 1ˢᵗ Book

The Orthodontist's Wife

GIDEON ELLIOT
Submission Erotica

HASKELL NELSON was the kind of boy mothers want their daughters to marry. He was polite, friendly, intelligent—although not too intelligent, not one of the abstract and arrogant brainy ones. He was not an intellectual. He came from a respectable family and had respectable prospects himself. He was a hard worker, had held a job all through high school, sung in the church choir, was on the tennis team, and didn't go nuts on weekends.

After two years at State College, he knew he was going to be an orthodontist. He was not the kind of boy, as the saying goes, who might make a woman feel like a million dollars, but there was an awfully good chance that after twenty years—maybe even ten—he would have a million dollars. Mothers whose daughters married a boy like Haskell Nelson could sleep satisfied. But, then, they wouldn't have to sleep with him. Their daughters—but this was seldom in their thoughts—longing for something more than split-level somnolence, might find their sleep less satisfying.

It was not surprising, then, that Harriet Baker was delighted when Haskell came over one Sunday afternoon carrying a bouquet of flowers "for the house" to tell her and Warren that he had proposed to their daughter Jody—everyone called her Bunny—and was seeking their blessing. They took out the bottle of Spumonti they had been given at Christmas but never opened, and Warren got four long stem glasses from the high shelf in the pantry and Harriet washed them, and they toasted the couple's future.

Jody was a bunny, pug nosed, blonde, pudgy, sweet herself and plagued with a sweet tooth that kept her endlessly trying to stick to a diet. Haskell was a Teddy Bear, slightly overweight, too, and relatively hirsute back and front with a blackish thatch of hair poking out from his shirt at the throat and covering his back and shoulders. He needed to shave twice a day if he were to look well-groomed, and in his car he kept an electric shaver, which he plugged into the cigarette lighter when he drove to the mall from the medical center for lunch every afternoon.

He worked long hours, and they decided that Bunny would do a four-hour shift every day, till lunch time, from nine to one in the office as receptionist/bookkeeper. It was not only good fiscal policy, but it gave them a sense of common enterprise. Afternoons, she kept house, went shopping, prepared dinner, which they ate later than most families in Hathaway Estates, at nine, half an hour after Haskell got home.

Almost immediately they tried to make a baby, and that was the impetus for their nocturnal embraces. But after more than three years, although his practice was going very well and they had easily managed to move from a ranch to a large colonial, they were still childless. Tests showed nothing wrong with him or his capacity to produce sperm, and Bunny felt a diminution in her value as a woman when she learned of her own infertility.

He was comforting and did not recriminate. Why should he? There was no fault, only misfortune. Nevertheless and surprisingly, Bunny found herself irritated by a suppressed resentment towards him. His never getting angry bothered her. Even though it would have been irrational, showing some anger would have shown that he'd had a real desire for a child, just by his expression of frustration over its having been thwarted.

Bunny, of course, felt guilty about her grievance, for holding his kindness, his temperateness against him. What! Did she really want a husband who made her life bitter when she was already pained? She knew it was her problem and best she'd better get rid of it or it would poison the well of their entire marriage. After all, they could adopt. He'd suggested it, in fact, before she'd even thought of it. But that gave her, strangely, just another cause for resentment and regret. It wasn't just having any old child. It was something about her body. It annoyed her he did not understand that. And she regretted her annoyance. How could he know how a woman would feel?

It was too much, and she realized she was not being fair. Her remorse made her affectionate and solicitous, and Haskell felt himself a blessed man to have a wife who bore a misfortune with the equanimity she displayed, and this happiness of his reinforced her angry resentment and her efforts to stifle it. Food, of course, was one of the ways, the major way, she controlled the beast of her discontent. She threw herself into gourmet cooking and into endless munching, and plump though she'd always been, now she began to be seriously overweight.

Typically, Haskell did not complain about her weight gain. She did, and he was solicitous. He was supportive in her dieting, and even lost a few pounds himself because of the new lower calorie meals she began to serve. This, too, was a bitter irony for her because she had no success at all in losing weight or in curbing her appetite. Her battle with her weight became the understood reason for the periods of frozen anger that began to appear and disturbed the apparent contentment of their marriage. After one of her "spells" she would apologize to him explaining how she was being driven crazy by an appetite she found it impossible to control even though she was struggling to do that. He always understood.

And then it came to him. A colleague had asked him why he wasn't using natural hypnosis instead of Novocain or gas for his patients. He'd answered that he doubted its effectiveness. His colleague demurred and invited him to go to a seminar on Hypnosis in Dentistry he'd been attending to see what a powerful and effective tool hypnosis actually could be. Haskell had no objection and was astonished at how completely wrong he'd been and how strongly the hypnotist could alter attitudes, perceptions and sensations, especially after he saw an actual root canal performed on an actual patient by an actual dentist using only hypnosis as an anesthetic.

It was while driving home reflecting on what he'd seen and when he determined to sign up for the course and use hypnosis in his practice that he thought of Bunny's weight problem. That, surely, where everything else had failed, might well be amenable to hypnosis. Why not? It was worth a try. When he got home and he recounted his day, he told her he thought maybe she ought to try hypnosis.

She was reluctant, expressed doubt, joked about being made to quack like a duck, but ultimately said she would try it, agreeing that it couldn't hurt and that it might do some good.

***

MAX FRANZEK was in his sixties, tall, wiry, eyes gray, like Homer's dawn, simultaneously magnetic and distant, a head full of thick iron gray hair, a firm jaw, strong teeth still deeply planted in healthy gums, a craggy face, and a tender smile of absolute acceptance. Bunny felt comfortable in his presence the moment she walked in and was drawn easily into his orbit. She told him she was at her wits end because she was trying to lose weight but was only gaining more no matter what she did and that her husband suggested she try hypnosis.

He looked at her with an uninterrupted gaze as he listened. As she spoke her words began to slur and she floated into the sphere of trance. In his rich east European baritone he told her she was becoming smaller and smaller and that soon nothing would remain of her except that part of her that wished only to obey his commands. She knew that was the only part of her that was true and she was eager to become his obedient slave. She knew she wanted him to be her master.

He asked her what was the matter and she told him she did not love her husband. He asked her why and she told him he was physically repulsive. He asked her if she wanted to be thin and she said she didn't care. He asked her if she wanted to be glamorous and she said she didn't care. He asked her if she thought she was beautiful and she said she was fat. He asked her if she wanted to feel sexually alive and she said she never had. He asked her why and she said she found it disgusting to give herself to her husband. He asked her what she wanted more than anything else and she said to surrender to a man who had the power to make her desire to give herself to him.

He told her that she was falling more deeply into a trance now, that whenever he said "Surrender," she would return to this trance state. He told her that when he woke her she would remember nothing. He told her that whenever he said, "I am going to offer several suggestions," she would find it easy to obey every one of these commands and impossible not to.

"I'm going to offer several suggestions," he said when she was awake. She was smiling because she felt relaxed. "First, you will no longer have any craving either to binge or to snack. Second," he said, "you will drive over to the health and fitness club I've written down on this card and ask for Ted. He trained with me. He's first rate personal trainer and a master hypnotist. I suggest you begin working with him on a daily basis. When you see him, you will say, 'My word is "Surrender,"' and after you do that, you will forget that you did, but every time Ted says the word, 'Surrender,' you will fall into the same deep trance you were in with me today."

She felt a glow of energy and said thank you Dr. Franzek. She gave him eighty-five dollars and set off for the fitness club to meet Ted. It couldn't have been more perfect if it had been a movie. She got off at a particularly woodsy exit of the Merritt Parkway, drove for a little while until she approached a chalet or a chateau. She wasn't sure which was the right word, but it was a large brick and timber mansion with turrets and gables and lead cased gothic windows on beautifully kept grounds that were obviously tended by a very fine nurseryman.

The rough flagstone path led up to an oaken double door that could have served as the portal to a carriage house. Inside the carpets were plush red. The receptionist sat behind a large oak desk. She stood up and came forward from behind the desk when Bunny entered. She was an attractive girl with a curvy figure dressed all in red—red suede heels, a red miniskirt and a red silk shirt open at the throat revealing a delicate neck and prominent collar bones.

Bunny stammered that Dr. Franzek suggested she come and that she see Ted. The receptionist smiled warmly and told her that she knew all about it, that Dr. Franzek had called ahead, that Ted would be out soon, but if Bunny would have a seat she'd like to get her a cup of herbal tea. Bunny thanked her, accepted the tea and sipped it slowly, savoring the warmth, only then realizing that a chill had indeed crept into the autumn day.

Ted was made to order for the place. He was drop dead good looking. There's no other way to say it even if it is a cliché. Bunny ought to have shrunk in such a presence, but she was aware of a calmness that she couldn't explain: Dr. Franzek's recommendation? The soothing tea?

At any rate she stood, offered her hand. His palm was dry and smooth and warm, and from it flowed a gentle and invigorating current. She knew she liked this man very much and was not alarmed that it might even be more than—she was married after all—she ought to.

But the thought slipped from her mind as Ted took her into a large room equipped like a gymnasium only far more luxuriously appointed than any gym she had ever seen in life or in the movies. She gasped.

"It is a good workout room," he said, smiling, enjoying her awe. He looked deeply into her eyes with his brown green eyes that were as deep as a forest. She smiled back as if aware that she was saying something of great importance and said without thinking, "My word is 'Surrender'."

"Surrender," he smiled. The word melted in her mind like honey and her eyes fell shut and he caught her as she slumped and gently said, "You can stand by yourself and you can open your eyes when you are in trance."

Her body regained its balance and her eyes opened although they were perfectly glazed and blank as if they were looking at something so far in the distant future that it was beyond what they could see. He felt a flood of excitement. His cock swelled.

***

LET US move the shot away from the immobilized pupils of Bunny's eyes now, tracking across the splendid scene of her transformation to Ted's oak desk which stands beneath the gothic window and its panes of leaded glass. The prospect is the autumn landscape. There is a calendar on the desk. The window is open, and the autumn wind, gently rustling the leaves of the grand maples—foliage that, as if by cinematographic special effect, bleeds from green to orange, gold and red, and then tumbles earthward leaving branches bare— the wind also rustles and then lifts and turns the leaves of the calendar revealing the tumbling days. Snow covers the branches and the landscape and January and February follow November and December until the cherry blossoms of April and the budding groves of May and June appear in the warm sunlight of the golden primavera.

By an intuitive sensitivity we recognize the lithe and bronzed body, well-wrought now and beautiful, in a thong bikini, emerging from a stream in the mountains beyond the chateau, shaking water from her long blond hair. She is glowing with health and freshness, and although she is only a fictional image, as we look at her now, we are drawn to caress her, to fondle her sweet, firm and high breasts, bowing before her, bringing our lips to them, feeling their fullness and warmth meet our pressing kisses. We want to press ourselves against her flat midriff, stroke her long legs and plant our kisses in obeisance on the firm flesh of her inner thighs.

She smiles as Ted takes her in his arms and pressing his lips to hers gently plays against them with his tongue while simultaneously caressing the mound of her vagina softly until the lubricating moisture of her inner desire draws his finger into her and she dances on its tip. "Surrender," he whispers.

"I do surrender, darling, master," she breathes the words and they mingle like embraces of the breath until she frees her lips from his command and slowly worships with her tongue the delicacy of his neck, and bows before the magnificence of his hard smooth torso, stopping by each nipple to suck from each the essence of her life, then passing the stony grandeur of his abdomen she kneels before him and slave to her desire and to his supreme mastery takes his iron cock into her mouth and holds his ball sac in her palm as if a priestess bearing a sacred vessel.

She rides his cock to the depth of her throat and takes him to a height where she knows she commands, and he becomes her slave until he, restored to power by withholding his orgasm even as her throat convulses as if it were a cunt, pushes her mouth away and tearing off her bikini slams his way inside so that there can be no doubt of his mastery and her dependency.

He rides her and she feels the pride of her submission and surrenders to him again and again with her every bucking movement, tearing at him with her kisses, gasping and losing her breath until flying like Pegasus she makes the final leap and her master pulls tightly on her bridal and with orgastic lashes brings her crashing into the shimmering sea where she floats upon her wings.

**

HASKELL FOUND himself again alone another evening after work, pursuing angry fantasies. He had suspended Bunny by the wrists with a taut rope, naked from a cross beam in the attic so that the tips of her toes nearly touched the floor, but not quite and they were immobilized by ropes that anchored them to spikes banged into the attic floor. He was dressed only in his sleeveless green scrubs and he was lashing her with a whip. She was crying, "Please forgive me, Haskell. I will try to become worthy of you." And he was laughing, calmly saying, "So now Bunny bitch, how do you like this transformation?" In actuality he was pulling at the flesh of his thick dick which was almost solid until the spill of semen fell from it and something hollow grew in him that tasted funny in his mouth and covered him with shame.

The ringing phone made him jump. It was Bunny calling to say she had extended her stay at the health farm for two more days but would be back when he got home Wednesday night, that she hoped he was enjoying his second bachelorhood and not being too naughty. Her silly teasing, so unlike the way the girl he'd married had spoken, and so far from an accurate perception of his state of mind, left him tongue tied and frustrated.

**

WEDNESDAY NIGHT, things went from bad to worse. Haskell still kept long hours, even though there was no financial need to. He had lived up to everyone's expectations with regard to his earnings. His practice was thriving, he had patented an improvement on a latex dental dam that had been bought by Dental Technologies for two and a half million dollars, and he made three-quarters of a penny on every dam sold.

This Wednesday night, however, he made it a point to get back even later than usual, not wanting to be the first one in the house if Bunny was late. Rather than be found waiting he wanted to keep her waiting. He stopped off after work at Benny's Annex, had a few drinks, traded cigars and cigar stories with Gus behind the bar and managed to drive home without being stopped by the cops. And still he got there before Bunny.

When he finally heard her key turning in the lock, his fury was contained but high. She sensed it, and she wanted no part of it. She gave him a quick peck with closed lips, and he grabbed hold of her wrists.

"Let go of my wrists right now," she said in a soft, cold, steady voice.

"What the hell has happened to you?" he shouted.

"What's happened to you?" she said, pulling her wrists free of his unsure grasp.

Her words—it surprised her too, but she heard it as clearly as he did—were not spoken in anger, nor were they a reproach, but a real question, the kind that recognizes the presence of the other. Somehow something, despite the involutions of desire, ego and betrayal—all types of desire, all types of betrayal—somehow something worthy of being called human had happened.

She had recognized, despite herself, it might be, that things were not as they ought to be with him. And he was, at that moment, haunted by the presence of something that was not present, not just by the burden of the world that was. He felt with a shudder the pull of a lost paradise, a desire for something that never had been but which he wanted with all his heart, even if he did not know what it was, and he began to cry. Grief, mixed with resentment, mixed with a need for pity, rushed out in sobs, and his fists clenched at he did not know what.

Her response, however, was disgust. She had no more desire to mother his weakness than to be the target of his anger. "Stop it," she said curtly.

Her words did stop him, as the elimination of oxygen stifles the life of a flame, and he was left in confusion, feeling neither his anger nor his grief but desperate incommunicable isolation.

End of the 2nd Book

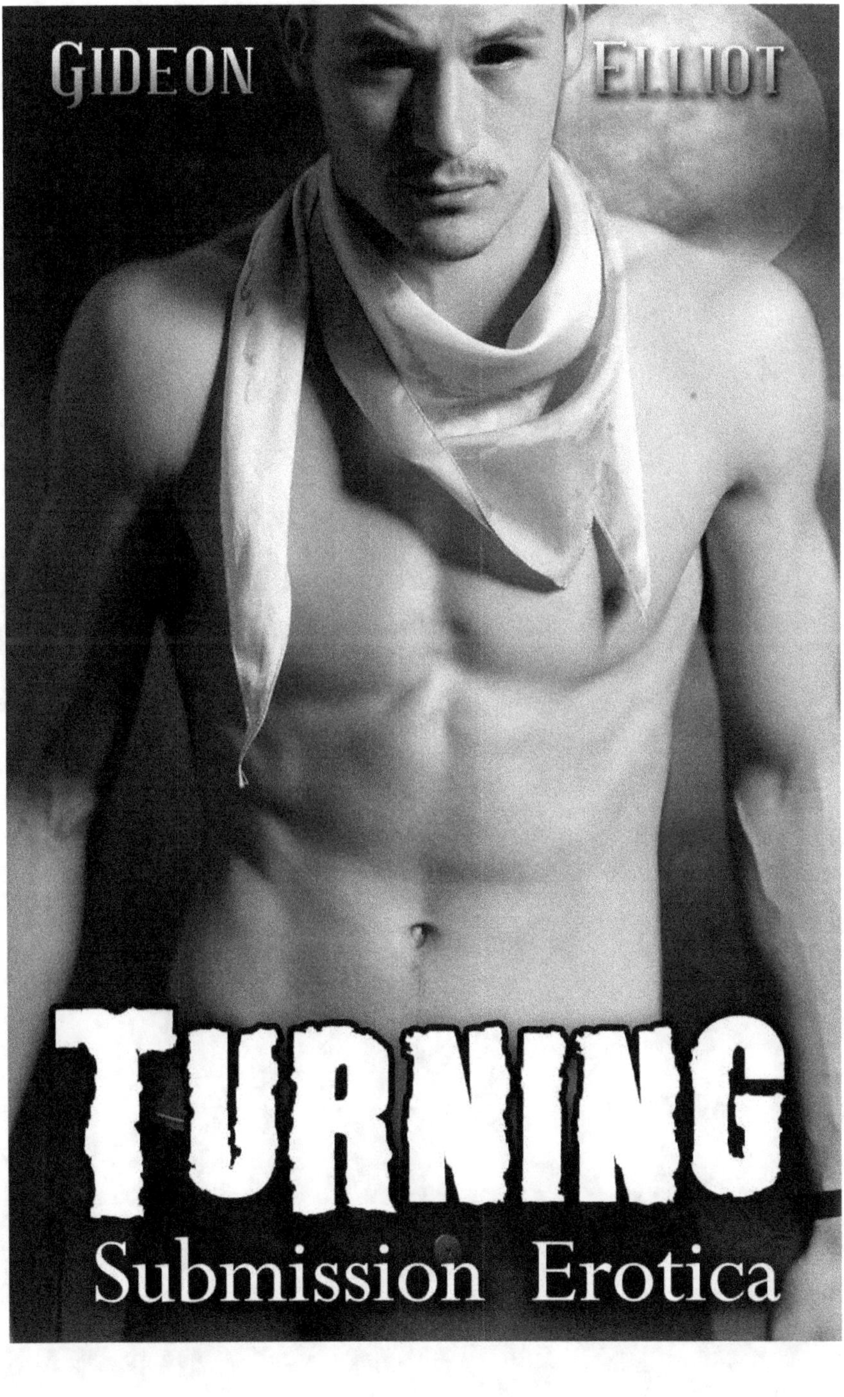
GIDEON ELLIOT
TURNING
Submission Erotica

"HOW MANY times can you talk about one fucking blow job?" Ned asked. They were sitting in Ned's place on Telegraph Avenue. Jeremy looked confused and distressed.

"I'm sorry," Ned shrugged, "but it's not like I haven't heard it before. I know. You were drunk. You were scared. You didn't want to do it. I believe you, and I'm not arguing with your feelings."

"It's easy to talk when you can't feel what somebody else feels," Jeremy said.

"Oh, don't be pathetic."

"I'm trying to talk about something very important to me, and you're insulting me."

"Something important to you! If that's all that's important to you, then everything else you're involved in has to be pretty trivial." Ned hadn't meant to be so severe, but he was fed up and frustrated. Since he'd run into Jeremy the week before last at the art institute, they'd been hanging around together. His hope of wooing him had pretty much been crushed under the weight of Jeremy's endless repetition of his "traumatic" drunken encounter with a gay man, when, "somehow," the night had finished off back in the guy's apartment and a round of sixty-nine. Big Deal!

"Fuck you," Jeremy cursed him.

"You wish," Ned returned it with a taunt.

"What's that supposed to mean?"

"You figure it out, pussycat." But Jeremy was in no mood to figure out anything, and charging at his interlocutor, broke his jaw and fled from the apartment.

"It isn't right," he said to himself repeatedly on his sullen trip across the country back to New Jersey.

***

HE TOSSED his duffel bag on the bed and stretched. He parted the curtains on the window and pulled up the blind. He looked out onto a backyard that was like an orchard. In the distance there was another house, as grand as his parents' house, the house that was there for him to come back to. They'd be back from Panama tomorrow. (What the hell were they doing in Panama? It wasn't to spend time on the beach.) So he had the whole house to kick about in by himself for the night. Good.

It was a good time to get a real feel of the place. He'd never live here again. At the end of the week he was moving into his own apartment in Greenwich Village. Not exactly his own. He'd have his own room and bathroom; he'd share the living room, kitchen, foyer, terrace with another guy.

They hadn't met, but the rental agent who put the deal together showed him the papers. Dalton Hambrode, what a name! He'd looked him up on the internet. His mother was Fanny Hambrode. What more did you have to know. He was doing graduate work at NYU in broadcasting. Jeremy was studying History and Political Science. He'd wanted to be a White House Adviser since he was nine and got interested in politics.

Mary Anne had been his girl in high school, and they saw each other at regular intervals during their time away at college. Now she came right over when he called. She was dressed her sluttiest, chewing gum and smoking a cigarette sticking out of a long black holder. She was leaning against one of the columns on the porch. He opened the door.

"Hey handsome, it's good to see you," she said, throwing herself at him and dissolving under him in one big kiss. He'd been prepared for this; he was bare-chested, wearing jeans, boots, and a chain with a St. Christopher medal falling on his smooth and well cut torso. "Come in," he said, breaking the kiss and leading her indoors.

"Come in yourself," she purred, running spidery fingers across his back. She is dark, Persian-looking and frisky as a cat. She growls and purrs simultaneously as he puts his hand on her inner thigh by her cunt -- that's how short her skirt is.

He sees her high heels and her firm well shaped legs, her well-muscled, tight bare midriff, her breasts, her luscious whore lips, her velvet violet eyes, and he clenches his palm around her sex. Then he enters her with his fuck-you finger to explore her with complete right of possession, as if he's got her sitting in the palm of his hand.

His parents were paying most expenses, but he had to find a job. His father thought it expedient that he not work in the bank presently. Avoid any...no need to go into it. Always keep an eye on the future! It's hard to know about the future, and it's good to be adaptable.

***

"NO, PLEASE, not Dalton. Danny."

"Danny," Jeremy said shaking hands.

Danny had arrived a few hours before. He was tall, well built with rugged good looks, sandy hair and irresistible eyes of blue. They looked around the apartment together, with Danny sizing up Jeremy, and Jeremy avoiding the glances toward Danny that kept trying to escape him. Both had seen the place before, but by themselves.

Now each had to absorb that it was not his but theirs. It would have to accommodate itself to them, and they were going to have to accommodate themselves to each other. There was an expanse of window facing west. The setting sun suffused the sky that filled their windows, and the broad expanse of the elephant-backed Hudson was below them, hardly flowing.

They went over to Bleecker Street and shared a hot, black-crusted pizza at John's. It was a blue sunny day. The people around them looked like they were doing things they wanted to do. It was a good world to be in.

"You really want to be a presidential advisor?"

"Yeah. So?"

"It's a funny thing to think of. To be a presidential advisor, like it's a career goal. But why not? Somebody winds up doing it."

"Me!" Jeremy said with over-confidence. "What about you? You want to be a broadcaster, right?"

"I want to figure out what's going on and tell everybody." Jeremy met his slice of pizza half way and nodded as he chewed. In Washington Square Park a passing boy smiled at them and Danny winked at him. Jeremy pretended that he didn't see. But Danny had a sense that there might be something dangerous about his roommate. Something told him this guy could fly off the handle.

"Television hypnotizes people," Jeremy said, challenging Danny.

"What's wrong with that?"

"It makes them into obedient consumers, robots."

"I think you're right about television, but is that what you think hypnosis is really about?"

"Yeah."

"Uh-uh, you're wrong. You talk about hypnosis like it's a message, but it's a medium, it's a method of focusing the attention and clearing the mind and making it receptive. What the mind actually receives…that's something else. If it's lies, subversion, and deceit or truth, openness, and support makes all the difference."

"You ever been hypnotized?"

"Yeah," Danny said.

"Really!" Jeremy said in surprise. "What's it like?"

"Very smooth, like falling asleep with the lights on so you know you're sleeping -- you know: you experience yourself sleeping even though you're asleep. It's not like you're dreaming, but like you're the dream. You become very graceful and easy going and good natured, blissfully compliant. It's cool. You never been?"

"No. Have you ever hypnotized anybody?"

"Quite a few times. How'd you think I pay for graduate school and a West Village apartment?"

"Your mother."

Danny didn't blench. He was used to it. "She's a big believer in independence and becoming yourself," he said. "I worked the Catskills and the Berkshires as a stage hypnotist for the past three summers. And I didn't use my mother's name, either."

Jeremy was stretched out on the futon in their common room making notes in his copy of Henry Kissinger's memoirs. His body was twisted uncomfortably but he forced himself not to notice. Danny had smoked a little and was sitting with headphones listening to the *Winterreise* and sketching cartoon images and trying to figure out captions.

"Hey Danny," Jeremy called out loud enough for him to hear. Lifting his ear phones, Danny turned to him.

"I gotta talk t' yuh. Now ok?"

"Sure. What's up?"

"I don't sleep. The girls I meet are boring. I'm restless. You think hypnosis could like maybe de-stress me a little?"

"Could."

***

AROUND THIS time, a guy in the film school Jeremy met was making a student film based on a short story by Julian Diener, and wanted Jeremy to be in it. It was a complex project. The film was going to be about twenty minutes long. The guy had already gotten somebody's apartment on the Upper West Side to shoot it in.

When they completed shooting, Marty, the guy who made the film, threw his arm around Jeremy, pulled him to him, loudly kissed him on the cheek and said, "You were terrific." And Marge, who lived with Marty, said "Why don't we go to the Grand Teccino for dinner?"

"You what?" Marty nearly howled when Jeremy told them he wanted to be the next Henry Kissenger.

"What's so funny?" Jeremy said, his temper flaring.

But Marty persisted. "This is a worthwhile thing to grow up to do?"

"What's wrong with it?"

"Go find out. And if you don't think it is wrong when you find out, you're not the same guy who played Derek all these last weeks.

"What's that supposed to mean?"

"Hey Jeremy, what's your sexual orientation?" Marge broke in, apparently from left field, changing the subject.

"Why do you want to know?"

"Well, if you're straight, I can have you, if you're gay, Marty can, and if you're bisexual, we both can."

Jeremy didn't like that this excited him, but it did. Still, he assured himself on his walk home, "I have will power and strength of character, and I gotta protect my future." So he'd said he really couldn't go home with them, that he had to study for finals bright and early. They looked at him like they knew he was lying, but they didn't say anything.

Jeremy wrote in his notebook:

I'm not stupid, and I'm not repressed. I know what was going on. Danny is a faggot. I can tell just by the way he looks at me. I guessed it the first day in Washington Square Park. Too bad for him. Nothin's gonna happen. But I still wanted to be hypnotized. I'm edgy. I'm getting headaches. I want to chill. I figure hypnotism could make me relax. I don't have to worry about becoming Frankenstein's monster or doing something I don't want. Hypnosis can't give anybody that kind of power except in the movies. So I'm not worried."

***

DANNY WASN'T surprised when Jeremy asked him to hypnotize him. But he was wary, and when he told him he would, he also told himself that he would proceed cautiously. And he did. He told him that he had to get himself prepped for it. They set a date - a week from the evening of their conversation, the next Wednesday. Jeremy was comfortably stretched out on the futon.

Relax Jeremy. Danny began and got into a slow and rhythmic induction until he had him. "What do you feel, Jeremy?"

"I feel good."

"Relaxed, easy, free of tension. What do you feel?

"Light? What do you feel?"

"I feel my chest. I want to press my chest to yours. I want to feel the hardness of your body pressing against me like stone."

Danny held himself back. He was not entirely surprised. He did not, however, expect so full-fledged an acknowledgement of desire, even in sleep, this soon, and he knew that it would evaporate with waking. Desire would sleep when Jeremy was awake and wake only in his sleep.

If Danny guessed right, avoidance of acknowledging anger was the cause of this disconnection. Jeremy experienced suppressing anger as well as sexual desire as a victory, anger at his sexual desire. And if he acknowledged anger, he'd have to acknowledge its cause.

***

GLISTERING SNOW covered New York and soon became grimy. It hadn't snowed for days, but the sun disappeared for almost a week and things were dismal, dingy and altogether dull. The fresh but already discarded pine and fir trees lined the curbs in front of houses all over the city declaring the gay times so fiercely anticipated already gone with nothing but uprooted trees and a nebulous sense of loss and waste remaining.

"This is not the spirit I need to be in," Jeremy thought, more consciously and painfully depressed than he had ever been, and unable to pull himself out of it. When Jeremy got home, Danny was a sight for his sore eyes. "Hey man," he said, "It's so good to see you. I have been so fucking down all day. It's good to see you. I was feeling so…I don't know, just…

"You're angry, Danny said.

"How do you know what I feel? I see you and I want you to take me in your arms and kiss me where it hurts and make me feel better. And instead you go at me, tell me I'm angry – like you're trying to pick a fight."

"But you do sound angry."

"That's because of you. I'm one way. And then you make me another. But I don't know why we're doing this, why we're talking about this when I just told you something important that you are entirely ignoring, like I didn't say it, which is like saying I don't exist."

You exist," Danny said, good-humoredly. And then he did something surprising. "Come here" he said drawing Danny to him and kissed me. Danny yielded. Then he drew back and looked at Jeremy. He blushed. And then their resistance snapped. Their lips met, then their tongues.

"You're going to regret this," Danny said.

"I won't," Jeremy said. "You have in the past."

"That was different. I was different. I was stuck. I was in a locked room, banging on the walls and beating at the door. But suddenly I feel out in the open. There's nothing I have to break out of. I just breathe.

"Like this" he said, kissing Danny.

The End

Here is a sample from another story you may enjoy:

5-BOOK BOX SET

Blue Identity

Gay Erotic Romance

GIDEON ELLIOT

There was nothing more I could do. He was gone and I knew there was no way I could bring him back. Perhaps that was a good thing. Perhaps it wasn't.

What I could do was take a shower, scrub myself down, shave, get dressed, go out and get a haircut, buy some new clothes, work out at the gym, go for a drink at Benny's, stop in at the new sushi place on Barrow Street, get home around midnight, get stoned, listen to Jauchtzet Gott in Allen Landen, the Schwarzkopf recording, jerk off, and get some sleep. Tomorrow morning I'd go into work.

It would keep me busy. It would keep me going. And that's really all that mattered after all.

* * *

Ellen was waiting for me on the doorstep when I got home.

"You look better than I expected," she said.

"What did you expect?"

"A wreck," she said.

"Sorry to disappoint you," I said.

"I'm not disappointed," she said. "I'm glad. Anybody after almost ten years..."

"What are you doing?" I said, quietly.

"What do you mean?"

"You know perfectly well what I mean."

It never failed. She was getting me angry. The last thing I needed. It was a trick of hers. But I caught myself in time.

"I don't want to do this, Ellen," I said with no affect.

"You don't want to do what?" she said.

She was baiting the hook. She'd use any response as a way into a fight. Fighting was foreplay for her. I wasn't having it, and I wasn't going to explain. Even that was a way of involving me. I wasn't even going to explain why I wasn't going to explain.

"Good night, Ellen," I said unlocking the door to the building.

"You don't know what's good for you," she said, on the verge of crying.

It wasn't going to work.

"Perhaps," I said. "But I'll deal with it. Good night." I let myself in and disappeared behind the door, closing it gently behind me, leaving her there.

Actually, I felt better than I thought I would.

If you enjoyed this sample then look for **Blue Identity**.

Also by this Author

A Second Chance

The Recruiter

A Furtive and Hidden Embrace

Diamond Shadows

Displacement

Keen Obedience

Between Two Thieves

Heart's Desire

Sensual Surrender

Erotic Aggression

Don't Forget You Love Me

Unstable Emotion

The Hazard Game

A Knight in the Forest

Captured Emotions

The Mesmerist's Tale

On His Own

The Good Bitch

Succumb Touch

Blue Identity

About the Author

Gideon Elliot was born in 1981 in Wichita, Kansas.

He grew up in San Francisco and spends the greater part of the year, now, on one of the Cyclades Islands in Greece where he runs a jazz café, paints, writes poetry, and swims.

He has a small apartment in Greenwich Village, where he stays from the middle of November to the end of April and, during those months, manages an erotic men's clothing shop. He began writing erotic fiction at the age of fifteen.

You may also like the books by these authors:

Dick Parker

Deckhands

Hot Gay Erotica

We locked through and got everything ship-shape. Our shift was almost over so when the B crew came on deck we went to the galley and ate some lunch. Cory and I went below.

"I think I'll have a shower," he said.

"Want someone to scrub your back?"

"Absolutely," he said.

We both stripped naked and walked to the shower. We turned on two spigots and took turns washing each other. We did our hair and then our bodies and of course we both were hard when we finished.

"How about a little rest?" Cory asked.

"I'm not real tired."

"Maybe we can just lay down."

I grinned and we hurried back to the room. Cory lay on his bunk on his back with his hard cock sticking up in the air. He put his arms up under his head and his armpit hair looked really sexy. I climbed onto the bed and knelt between his legs. I looked down at him and he looked so beautiful, he took my breath away.

"I can't believe I got so lucky to meet you," I said.

"The feeling is mutual Stew."

I leaned forward and took his cock in my hand and began to suck it. It was hard as steel and he closed his eyes and moaned.

"Oh man, that feels good."

I sucked on his balls and lifted them up and licked between his nut sack and his asshole. He shuddered when I did that and then he lifted up his legs. His butt hole was all pink and looked lovely. I leaned down and began licking it.

"Oh Stew, oh man," he whispered.

I reached up and pinched his nipples. He gasped.

"Stew, I want you to fuck me."

"Really? Hell yeah," I said.

"Get a condom from the dresser. Top drawer on the right."

I pulled the drawer open and ripped the wrapper open and rolled the condom down my cock.

"There's lube in there too."

I found the lube and lubed up my cock and his ass. I wiped my hand off on my wet towel.

Cory pulled his legs up to his chest and I put my dick up to his hole. I pushed and he moaned but my dick head slid in. His ass ring clenched my dick so I let it sit for a minute. He released the clench and I began pushing in a little at a time until I was slapping his ass with my nuts.

"Oh baby, that feels so good," he said.

I leaned down and we kissed. He sucked on my tongue. He wrapped his legs around my waist and we took our time and fucked for ten minutes. We were both sweating and panting when I felt the feeling.

"I'm about there," I said.

"Shoot it on my face," he said.

I grinned.

"Kinky," I said.

I fucked him for another minute and then I knew I was about to blow. I pulled out and ripped off the condom, straddled his body and jacked myself on his face. I came in three big squirts and then some more dribbled out. I held onto the bed post to take a breather.

"Oh man," he said.

"You need to get off Cory," I said.

"Yeah, I'm about to explode."

"Fuck me."

"Really? Sure as hell."

I got off him and he quickly put on a condom. My cock was limp and all full of cum so I knelt on the bed. He got behind me and lubed up my hole and then he slid his cock into me. Oh man it was a butt full.

"Oh Stew, you've got a hot ass kid."

We fucked for three or four minutes and he began to make a sound in his throat.

"Are you close?" I asked.

"Really close."

"Shoot on my face," I said.

I'd done it to him and it was hot. So why not have him do it to me?

If you enjoyed this sample then look for **Deckhands**.

Prisoner of His Heart

Hot Gay Romance

Chris Johns

I remember Toy being so proud that the King was the longest ruling monarch in the world, longer even than our Queen Elizabeth. We went to Pattya for some beach time and the wonderful fun filled gay area. We stayed in the Nippa Lodge, right on the beach. We played badminton, swam in the pool and the sea, and I sunbathed. Toy didn't; to him a dark skin meant "peasant," that is… someone who worked outdoors. He couldn't be confused with them, so he stayed under a beach umbrella and read; he was always reading. No doubt that was the reason he was so good at his course subjects. He never ceased to please me with his enthusiastic approach to life, always appearing to be happy, and I very quickly fell in love with him.

Both of us were almost virgins in sexual experience; we had both played around at school, but just normal boy/boy experimentation, so our lovemaking became a voyage of discovery for both of us. It was ages before we got beyond the basics of mutual hand jobs, and blowjobs were magical when they happened. The big one was a long time in coming… Toy was so small, and I was worried about hurting him. Eventually, he wanted it more than me so we tried it. The result was a bucket of tears from him, and a vow that he would be mine forever, now that I had taken his virginity. I'm sure every first timer says something similar so I didn't set much store by the words.

During my time in prison, I just hoped that he would find another lover to look after him in our big bad world. I determined as we drove towards Cambridge that I would use my time before college started to find out what happened to him. I had contact details for his sister, so if they hadn't changed I should be able to find out what I wanted to know.

I held my breath as the locksmith gained entry for me and stood back. I opened the door, and the first thing that struck me was the smell. It took me back to my childhood… days spent in the country roaming in the woods and fields on camping trips. It smelt of summer, lilacs, and freshly mown grass. I turned to my foreign office escort with a bemused look on my face.

He had picked up on it as well, having been informed that he might well have to take me to a hotel to start with. He just shrugged. From the entrance hall I walked into the lounge; it was neat and tidy, clean as a whistle, with fresh flowers on display, and looking round the walls I could see landscape posters of Thailand, all neatly framed. The remainder of the flat was the same…immaculate. The bedroom told me what my mind was finding hard to accept. On the bedside table was a picture of Toy and me taken at the Royal Palace in Bangkok the Easter of my visit, and on the other side a picture of his parents and sister. I sat down with a bump. Toy was still in residence, but how?

I recovered my composure and told my escort I would be fine. Not to worry about keys…I had the feeling they would appear sometime today; if not, I would telephone for the locksmith to return with a new lock. When they had gone, I rummaged around to see what else there was. The wardrobe and chest of drawers in the master bedroom were as before…all my clothes neatly hung and stored, all smelling fresh. They would, of course, be too big for me until I put my weight back, but that was going to save me a load of money replacing what I thought had been lost. The kitchen cupboards were full of Thai herbs and spices, lots of fresh food in the refrigerator and I noted a total lack of alcohol. Good boy…he hadn't changed. I sat back in the lounge and pondered why he was still here, four years, so he was twenty now to my twenty-three. He should have finished his course so why was he still in England?

It was late afternoon when I heard a key in the lock. I stood up and waited. He appeared in the doorway and saw me. I thought he was going to faint he looked so shocked. Neither of us moved for what seemed like an eternity before he suddenly burst into tears and fell to his knees.

"I'm sorry, I'm so sorry, please forgive me."

If you enjoyed this sample then look for **Prisoner Of His Heart**.

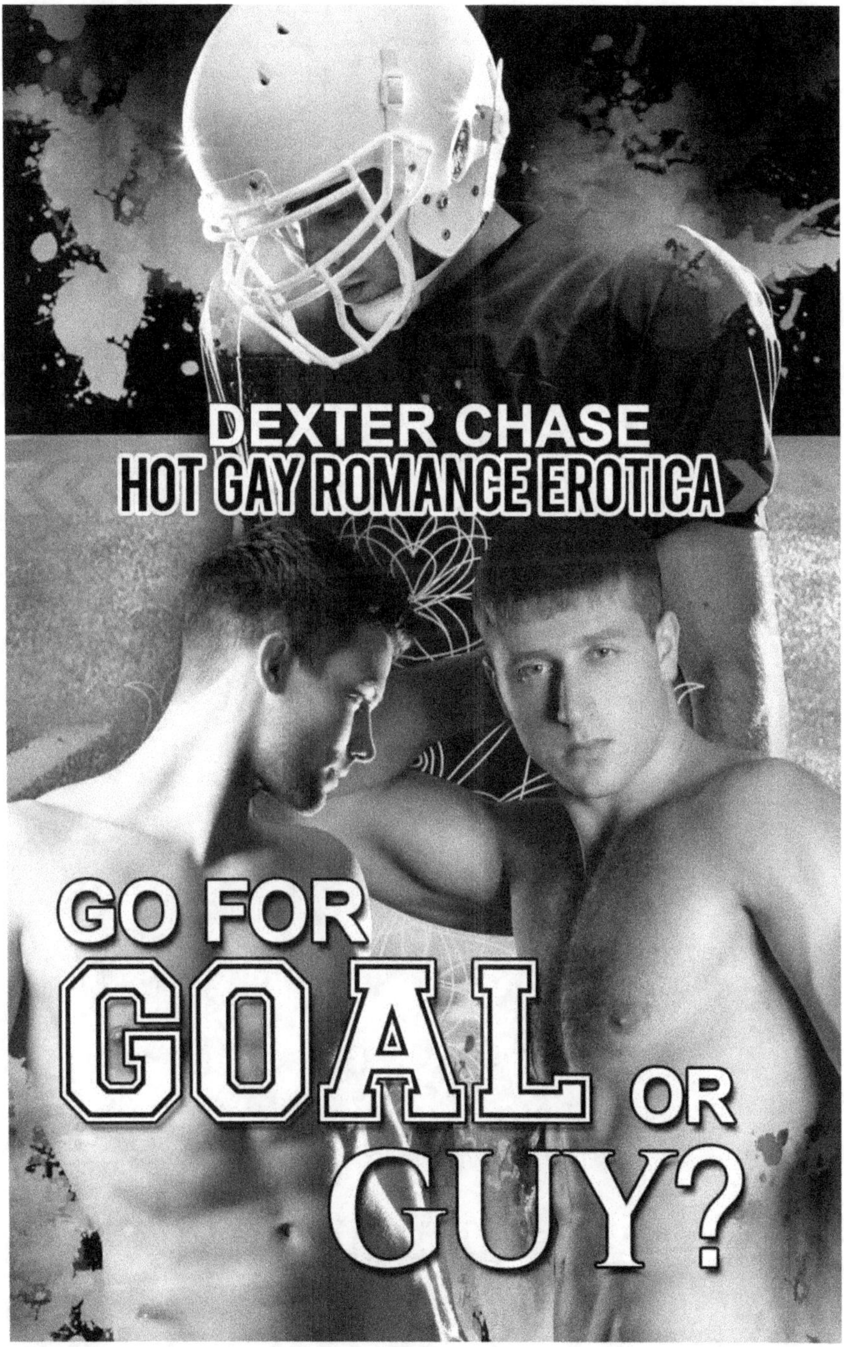
DEXTER CHASE
HOT GAY ROMANCE EROTICA
GO FOR
GOAL OR
GUY?

"Marcel, I'd like you to come with me to watch an academy game this afternoon"

That request was really the beginning for Luke Cross. He had been educated at a good private school, but Soccer was not played competitively so there were no inter-school matches for his talent to shine. In frustration he had played the occasional game for a local junior team. In his last season before graduating and sliding off to university Luke played for this team in a home match.

Tom Anders Jr. was a football freak and when his dad was home at a weekend, a rarity because Tom Sr. was a scout for Premier League team, Bedfont Rovers, he would drag him off to watch the local team play. On this Saturday, Tom sat mesmerized by the incredible skill of Luke Cross. The score was an embarrassing 16-0. Luke had scored 12 and assisted the other 4. It was a performance that had Tom's blood pulsing at an incredible rate. He collared the boy before he disappeared at the final whistle and made an appointment to call on him and his parents that evening.

"Luke, Mr. and Mrs. Cross, I won't beat about the bush. I think Luke is an amazing talent and I would like to sign him to the Academy at Bedfont. Unless I am very wrong he will be offered a seniors contract by the time he is 18."

The Cross family were blown away and once it was accepted that Luke would be tutored so that he sat his A Level exams on time a contract was signed.

"A car will come for you on Tuesday Luke. That will give you the chance to clear all your gear from your school and say your goodbyes."

When Tom had left, Luke's father sat down to talk with his son.

"What are you going to do about your sexuality, Son?"

"I'll have to keep it hidden Dad, at least until I'm an established player, maybe even forever. I'll do it if I can play soccer at the top level."

"Good boy, but now you understand why I wanted you to finish school. University can be put on hold and you can take up a place in years to come if necessary."

Luke gave his dad a hug and with tears in his eyes spoke to both parents.

"I was so lucky when parents were handed out. I got the best friends I could ever wish for."

Understanding was not an adequate word to describe the Cross's. Luke had talked to his dad about his sexuality when he was fourteen. He didn't understand the feelings he had about other boys. Sex education had talked about boy/girl sex, nothing about gay sex, and Luke hadn't been confident enough to bring up the subject. His father had given him enough detail for his curiosity to peak and he had explored on the internet. A year later he had his first gay experience when he and a friend had jacked off together, followed a while later by doing each other. Things hadn't progressed beyond that but Luke wanted to try blowjobs and anal. His father had accepted it when Luke had confirmed he was gay.

"I'm sorry, Dad, however much I try, thinking about girls doesn't do anything for me, but I spend half my life erect thinking about boys."

"I guess we don't have much choice deciding who we find sexy, Son. I think that is decided at birth. Just make sure you are careful, legal doesn't mean accepted."

That was how it was left and Luke became comfortable in his skin, knowing that he would have a difficult ride if his sexuality ever became known but also knowing he would always have the support of his parents.

The Tuesday morning was the start of a meteoric rise to prominence. Luke was coached at Bedfont Youth Academy for nearly six months until he had sat his A Levels and celebrated his 18th Birthday.

"Luke, Tom wants you to play in the reserves match this evening."

Tom had approached the manager of the senior squad and persuaded him to watch the reserve team match.

"Marcel, you can have my resignation if you think I have wasted your time at the end of the match."

That was good enough for Marcel Verona, Tom was the most successful scout he had ever worked with.

They watched the full 90 minutes with Marcel's mouth hanging open in shock at the performance of Luke Cross.

"I want him in my office first thing in the morning Tom. Has he got an agent yet?"

If you enjoyed this sample then look for <u>Go For Goal Or... Guy?</u>.

Our First Meeting

The Notebook

D.D. WATSON

He searched for shelter having no clue where to turn. Exposed to the world and vulnerable, skin damp and sprinkled with dirt from running through the woods.

The forest was dense and had no visible trails; the sun was going down and the entwined branches blocked out what little light he had. Tears welled in his eyes, but he fought them back refusing to show any form of weakness.

He found shelter in a cave that was for now, his only refuge; he fled from his captors or maybe; they let him escape? He wrapped his arms around his shivering body as he kneeled down to the ground exhausted from the run he had to endure on barefoot. His body screamed from the torments; only moments ago inflicted on him...

***

Arian Taylor-Kinney, nicknamed Rin by his fathers, scribbled hastily in his notebook the story that burned in his head. A college student with brilliant soft golden-brown eyes, long auburn hair that shaped his soft face and seemed to obey as it drifts across his magnet eyes when he read or smiled with his curvy lips. His trim built helped draped his clothing that usually was just tee shirts and jeans. Arian hasn't had experience in relationships, sexual or monogamy. He was homeschooled by his father from pre-school to the last day of high school.

When entering college he wasn't as overwhelmed with his academics as he and his parents predicted, socializing was a bit different, but not problematic he has been to different groups where he'd made friends growing up, dance, soccer, swimming, and theater.

During his first semester he mostly focused on finding his classes, having to share his views in front of strangers, appointments, lectures, and due dates.

He bypassed moving into the dorms something his fathers disapproved. Arian reasoned that they lived close to the campus and that he would make friends just as easy commuting back and forward and that it would just be a waste of money.

As he settled into his second semester, he began to notice other people who were interested in him, males and females. Arian didn't want to be distracted from his studies, so he made friendships but nothing more. To tame the growing urges he had from the offers he was receiving from his classmates, mainly the males, he continued a method he performed back in high school to write his desires down in spiral notebooks.

The fantasies detail in location, positions; the men involved and the level of heat they were performing. Arian spilled his darkest, purest desires out on the line paper and what started with one notebook turned into more. He even came across a muse that seemed unreal, but he did become Arian's star player in most of his fantasies.

Sitting outside was a joy for him because during his younger days, and on nice weather his father performed a few of his lessons at the park or in their backyard. On this one particular day, Arian enjoyed relaxing alone on a bench under the shade of trees while writing and watching passersby.

"Hey Arian," said a tall blonde male who sat beside him as if he was a close friend. His physique was impressive showing through his close-fitting tank top and shorts as he put his arm behind Arian's shoulders resting it on the bench. Staring at the brawny arm, Arian wondered if he could dodge it—if his interloper decides to embrace him.

"Sorry, do I know you?" he asked leaning forward closing his notebook and grasping it firmly in his lap.

"Sure you do— Peter we have the same English class, Professor Law?" he smiled a familiar smile that Arian's become accustomed to. The same grin that said more behind it than it presented. His hand dropped to Arian's upper back, he tensed up and tried to shift away.

"I'm sorry I'm pretty sure I would remember you." Peter leaned closer placing his free palm on top of Arian's whom gripped his notebook even tighter.

"Well to be honest you always had your head in a book or writing something in that notebook but I did make it my business to sit nearby you and ask for a pencil."

"That was you?"

"Yes and it hurts my feelings that you don't remember me."

"Sorry, Professor Law had a lot of notes to take down, and he had asked me to use my notes as a class reference," Arian lied.

"Well, you can make it up to me." His fingers slid down Arian's spin sending heated tension throughout his skin.

"I can?" Arian shifted again and managed stop the message the sensation was sending to his cock.

"Dinner at my place," said Peter, who ignored Arian's evading.

"Your place?"

"Yeah, I have an apartment, my parents' ideal to help me study," he said looking Arian over intently as he moved his fingers from his back to reach around and touch his face.

"Is it helping?" Arian asked turning his face to avoid Peter's touch on his cheek only to get caught locking eyes with his green orbs. Peter managed to catch Arian's chin and hold his gaze.

"Well, why don't you come over with your notes and you can test me?"

"Well I—"

Just before Arian was about to turn him down a male student ran up to them grabbing Peter's arm.

"Peter you need to come quick."

"Not now Sam, I'm busy," he snapped keeping his attention on Arian.

"But your car." That did it; Peter leaped from the bench and fixated his full concentration on Sam.

"What about my car?"

"All the tires are missing."

"What?!"

"Also the engine."

"Are you kidding me?"

"Go see for yourself."

Peter darting away, Sam remained behind as Peter raced off and turned to Arian, who was standing collecting his things to head to class.

"Where you headed?" asked Sam. Arian looked at him with a puzzled look.

"To class."

"Aren't you concerned about Peter's car?"

"It's none of my business."

"That's not what I saw a moment ago you two looked quite comfy."

Arian wasn't skilled in relationships but did know when someone was jealous.

"Look, I scarcely knew Peter until now so whatever—this is," he gestured with his hand. "He's all yours."

"Damn right he is. I see what you do to men," he snapped, stomping off.

"What did he mean by that?" thought Arian, as he walked to his next class.

A young male watched the scene with full concentration as if he was watching a play. He held a can of unopened soda between his ring-covered fingers. As Arian walked away, Sam approached him.

"All better?" he asked taking the soda from him.

"Yeah thanks, I owe you."

"So you'll cover for me at work on Saturday?"

"Can do."

"Thanks Cross you're a life saver," he said popping the cap and taking a deep swallow.

"No, you are," replied Cross, gathering his messenger bag that strangely resembled Arian's that Sam noticed.

"Hey, I know it's none of my business but if you like him then just tell him."

"I couldn't handle the rejection."

"Cross you're beautiful, if you weren't so into him I'd ask you out."

"But I am into him and—I would like to handle it in my way."

If you enjoyed this sample then look for **Our First Meeting**.

Here Comes Trouble

Becoming Gay Erotica

ANGUS MacGREGOR

Sitting on this ridge top, I wonder why in the hell I ever agreed to come on this elk hunt. I don't really even like hunting. I used to, but not so much anymore. I mean, I love the camaraderie, and being outside in Oregon, and the beer. I love the beer the most. The whiskey is pretty great as well. I love the way the mist and clouds hug the mountains of the coast range like an old lady wearing a fur. The carpet of endless green, an ocean of Douglas fir that slides down the hills and tucks in and around rock outcroppings and pulls up its skirts for the rivers to splash through. The smell of wood smoke and the crisp autumn air that is just waiting to turn blue and bathe the mountains in frigid winter. But something is up with this hunting trip. It has been strange since the minute we got on the road. What am I saying? It's been weird for months.

Now that I am paying attention, and if I am honest, it's been going on since Emma and I met back in college. I dreaded the whole – "meet the parents" thing. I'm a real outgoing guy, not shy in the least. I don't have any confidence issues either. I mean, I'm lucky enough to have good looks and the kind of personality that most people seem comfortable with. But it's different meeting the parents. There's a whole other level of scrutiny and judgment that be part of that.

But I should back up, because this story began months before that, shit, it was years. I was the baby of my family, Chad Alonzo Martinez. A big brown-eyed, black haired, tanned little ball of energy. I had a brother that was ten years older than me. I adored him, but he and I had zero in common and hardly spent any time together at all. I was barely in grade school when he was graduating from high school. I did get to spend about a year in his bedroom before he moved out. See, I had a sister too, and she and I had shared a bedroom for quite a while, but as she got older, she was done with having a younger brother in the middle of her business. Jack said he didn't mind, which looking back, I find hard to believe. He was practically a grown man and I was just this cute little boy. But back then, I went to bed so early, he was rarely in the room with me. He came to bed way after me and I was always up and out of the room before he starts stirring since he didn't have a first period class.

There were a few nights I woke up in the middle of the night to look over and see him stroking his cock fast and furious. I knew better than to interrupt something so obviously private. But I would lay still and watch in fascination as his hand moved silently up and down his huge penis. His eyes would close and he would fondle his balls, belly, and nipples as he jacked. A few times, I even saw him seemingly slide a finger up his ass, which was both mystifying and utterly shocking at the same time. In the end, he would raise his furry ass off the mattress and send a fat rope of semen blasting up on his hairy chest and belly. He would usually grab some scandalously grimy cum rag from underneath the bed and wipe off his chest and then turn over and begin to snore. I had no idea what the whole thing meant, but it was fascinating nonetheless. A few years later, I followed in his footsteps and began rubbing one off every night before sleeping, secretly thinking my older brother for the lesson he didn't even know he was providing.

There were a few conversations that also contributed to my sexual education. Jack tended to take really long showers, probably because he was masturbating the whole time in there as well. Very often, I would be brushing my teeth or taking a little boy dump when he would open up the curtain and step out of the shower in all his muscled, hairy glory. Most often, his penis would be still erect and I would watch astonished as it bobbed and bounced on top of impossibly huge testicles. Several times he caught me watching and made a point to walk over and rub my face in his crotch, playfully, but all the same, shocking for a little kid. Sometimes he would reach down and grab my penis or nuts and give them a playful squeeze and say, something ridiculous.

"Damn, little bro, your dick is almost as big as mine. You are gonna be hung like a horse by the time you are in high school."

If you enjoyed this sample then look for **Here Comes Trouble**.

WANT FREE COPIES OF MY BOOKS?
Just visit my blog and download free copies of my books:
http://gideon-elliot.awesomeauthors.org/gideon-elliot/